Look and Find®

MARVEL

AVENGERS

we make books come alive™

pi kids® **Phoenix International Publications, Inc.**

Chicago • London • New York • Hamburg • Mexico City • Paris • Sydney

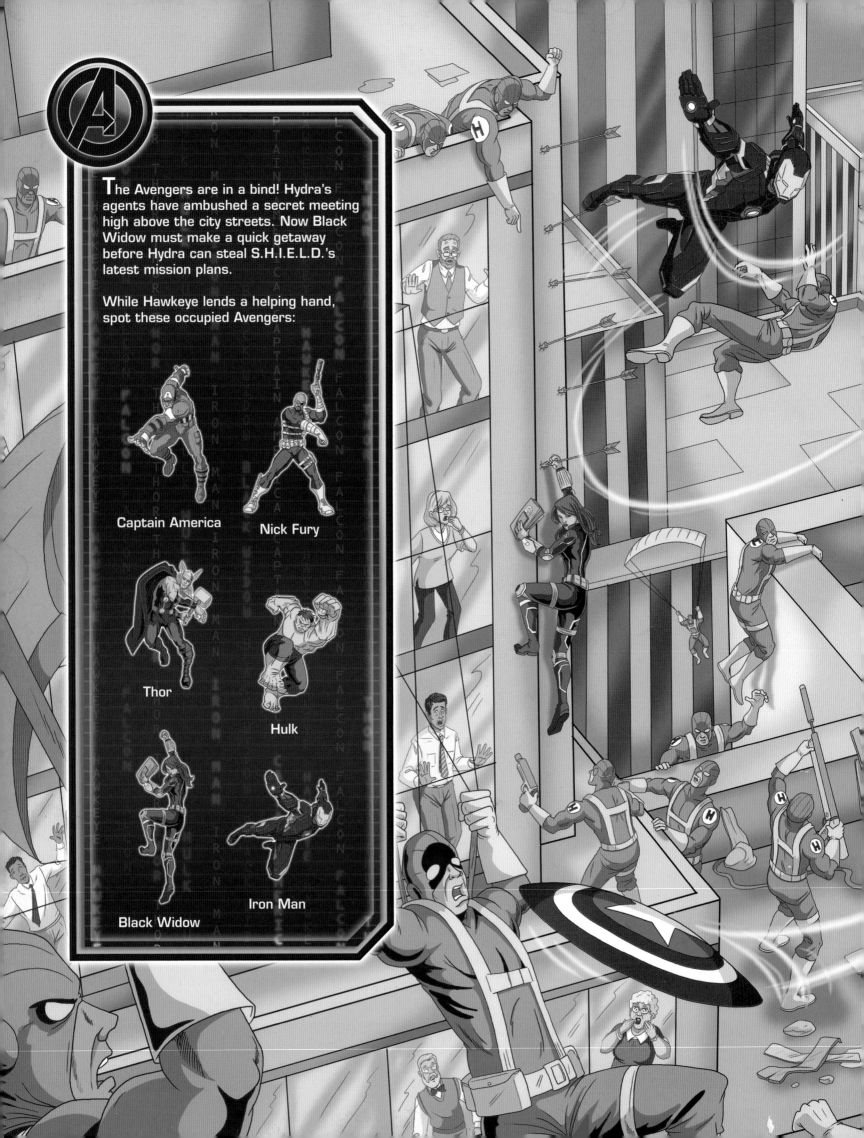

The Avengers are in a bind! Hydra's agents have ambushed a secret meeting high above the city streets. Now Black Widow must make a quick getaway before Hydra can steal S.H.I.E.L.D.'s latest mission plans.

While Hawkeye lends a helping hand, spot these occupied Avengers:

Captain America

Nick Fury

Thor

Hulk

Black Widow

Iron Man

Black Panther is caught between a helicopter and a hard place! As he takes on Klaw's airborne emissaries, Falcon soars to his rescue.

While the dauntless duo defends Wakanda, scan the skies for these unwelcome henchmen:

Tony Stark is enjoying the Fourth of July spectacle from atop Avengers Tower... when an unexpected guest suddenly drops in to extinguish the celebration.

As Tony dons his Iron Man suit to battle the Crimson Dynamo, look for these dazzling aerial displays:

On their way to Avengers HQ, Ant-Man and Wasp are sideswiped by Whirlwind! The pint-sized duo tries to lose their adversary in a birthday bonanza...but they get more than they bargained for.

While Ant-Man and Wasp dodge candles, cake, and caffeinated kids, look for these birthday items:

taffy

gumdrop

this candle

this lollipop

this party hat

this party horn

this licorice whip

this balloon

The moviegoers at the local theater are excited for the new Super Hero film premiere. When Vision makes a surprise appearance, everyone agrees: these special effects are the most realistic yet!

As Vision pursues his nemesis, Ultron, spot these surprised spectators:

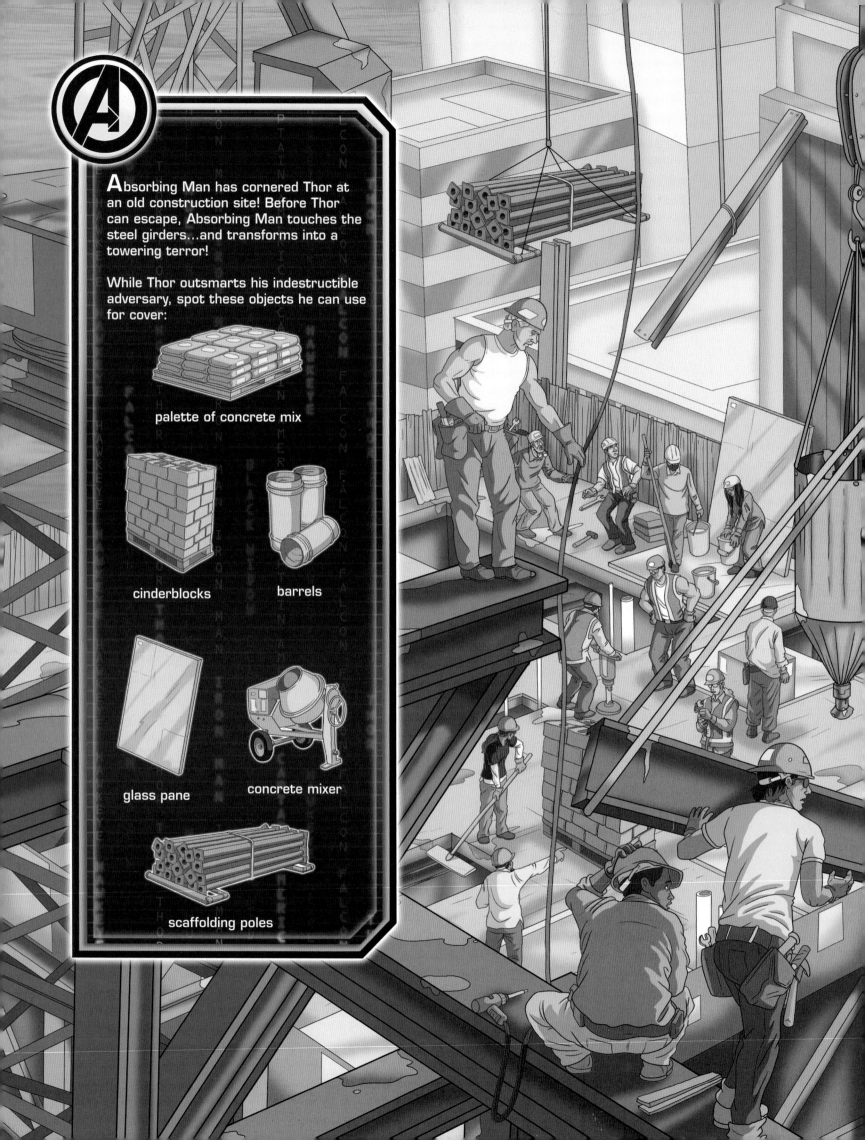

Absorbing Man has cornered Thor at an old construction site! Before Thor can escape, Absorbing Man touches the steel girders...and transforms into a towering terror!

While Thor outsmarts his indestructible adversary, spot these objects he can use for cover:

palette of concrete mix

cinderblocks

barrels

glass pane

concrete mixer

scaffolding poles

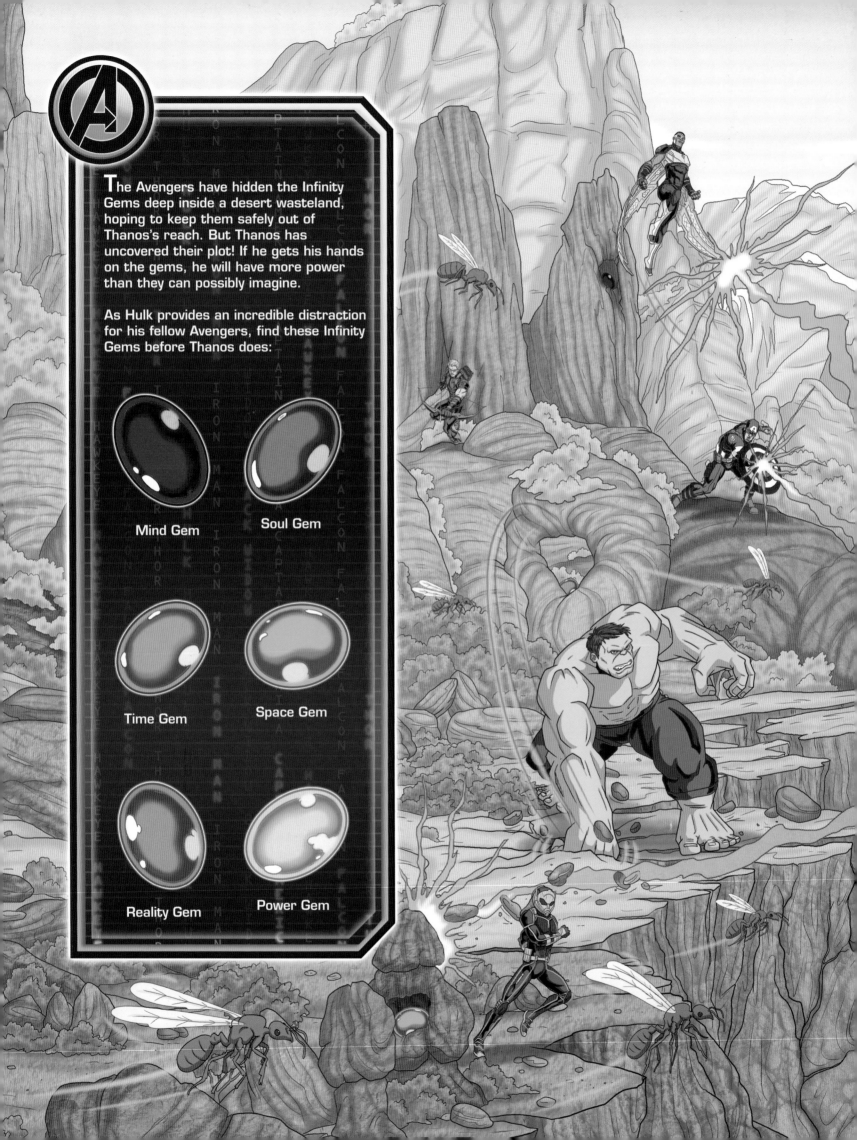

The Avengers have hidden the Infinity Gems deep inside a desert wasteland, hoping to keep them safely out of Thanos's reach. But Thanos has uncovered their plot! If he gets his hands on the gems, he will have more power than they can possibly imagine.

As Hulk provides an incredible distraction for his fellow Avengers, find these Infinity Gems before Thanos does:

Mind Gem

Soul Gem

Time Gem

Space Gem

Reality Gem

Power Gem

The Avengers have worked hard to earn a much-needed day off. They spend it at the fair, doing what they each do best.

As the Avengers reward themselves for saving the universe, point out these safe and happy (and surprised!) fairgoers:

cool cucumber

ring-toss virtuoso

patron of the arts

bad-luck bumper car operator

star-struck sister

aspiring boxer

popcorn-loving passerby

Sneak back to the secret S.H.I.E.L.D. meeting and look for these concerned citizens:

handyman in over his head

concerned crossword enthusiast

tenant behind on beauty sleep

hotel guest with a view

CEO thinking "OMG!"

banker with high interest

granny missing her soaps

Warp back to Wakanda and find these features among the foliage:

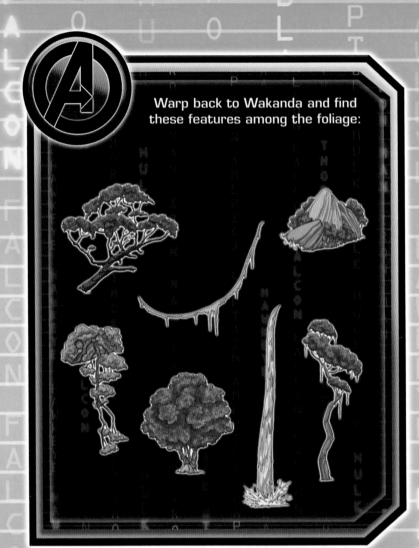

New York City shows its patriotism by celebrating the Mighty Avengers! Soar back to Avengers Tower and spot the fireworks displays shaped liked these Avenger weapons:

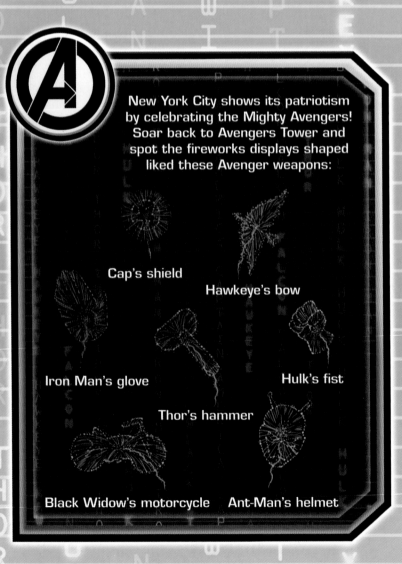

Cap's shield

Hawkeye's bow

Iron Man's glove

Hulk's fist

Thor's hammer

Black Widow's motorcycle

Ant-Man's helmet

Ant-Man isn't the only one enjoying the warm spring air. Buzz back to the birthday party and spot these other busy bugs:

beetle

butterfly

wasp

this ant

caterpillar

dragonfly

Buy another ticket to the Super Hero movie so you can munch on these cinematic snacks:

soda

nachos

hot dog

pretzel

this popcorn

this candy

chocolate bar

Quick! Charge back to the construction site and find these crew members racing for cover:

Nervous Nathan

Handy Henry

Befuddled Frannie

Startled Seymour

Distracted Deborah

Crouching Kevin

Tough Tina

Bolt back to the epic battle with Thanos and find these intergalactic heroes saving the day:

Black Widow

Iron Man

Hawkeye

Thor

Captain America

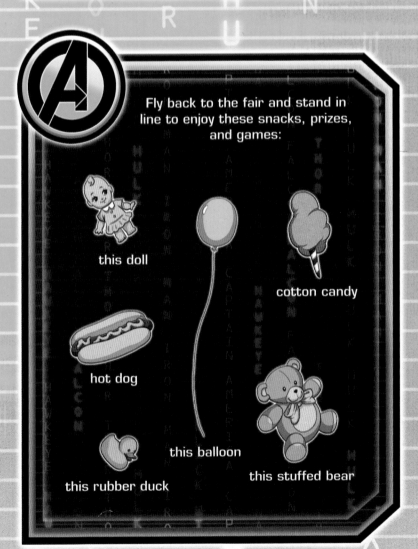

Fly back to the fair and stand in line to enjoy these snacks, prizes, and games:

this doll

cotton candy

hot dog

this rubber duck

this balloon

this stuffed bear